Something about this disturbed him greatly.

New York's financial district. Three major attacks that he knew of: this one in 1920, the 1993 bombing of the World Trade Center, and the 2001 destruction of the World Trade Center.

Were they all time-guarded events? If so, were they time-guarded by Homeland or Justice or the Time Department? Or by someone else? Something else?

Lane stood up slowly.

He had to make a choice here.

He could remain the ignorant figurehead, or he could step into his role as the chief investigator of time irregularities for the Federal Government.

He'd allowed others to dictate policy during his first six months here.

Time to change that, no pun intended.

ALSO BY
KRISTINE KATHRYN RUSCH

THE RETRIEVAL ARTIST SERIES

Writing as Kris Nelscott

THE SMOKEY DALTON SERIES

A Dangerous Road

Smoke-Filled Rooms

Thin Walls

Stone Cribs

War at Home

Days of Rage

Street Justice

AND

Protectors

———

Writing as Kristine Grayson

The Charming Trilogy, Vol. 1

The Charming Trilogy, Vol. 2

The Fates Trilogy

The Daughters of Zeus Trilogy

SEPTEMBER AT WALL AND BROAD

KRISTINE KATHRYN RUSCH

September at Wall and Broad

Copyright © 2014 by Kristine Kathryn Rusch

First published in *Fiction River: Time Streams*, edited by Dean Wesley

Smith, WMG Publishing, August 2013

Published by WMG Publishing

Cover and Layout copyright © 2014 by WMG Publishing

Cover design by WMG Publishing

Cover art copyright © Rolffimages/Dreamstime

ISBN-13 (trade paperback): 978-1-56146-893-5

ISBN-13 (hardcover): 978-1-56146-894-2

SEPTEMBER AT WALL
AND BROAD

MANHATTAN
SEPTEMBER 16, 1920

SHE DIDN'T WANT to go to work this morning. Normally, Philippa couldn't wait to leave the tiny two-room walkup she shared with five other women. The place smelled of grease and dirt so old that no amount of bleach would get it out. She had tried to clean the flat when she realized she would have to live like everyone else in this godforsaken century. She scrubbed the place until her hands were raw, and made no difference whatsoever.

Ambition was cold comfort when you shared a mattress with two other women—girls in 1920 parlance— neither of whom had bathed in the last week. The flat had two windows, both of which overlooked the brick building next door. No breezes, no sunlight.

Not that it mattered. She stayed out of the flat as much

1

as she could, coming back to sleep and change clothes. She probably smelled no better than her companions. The bathroom was down the hall, the bathtub foul, and the toilet an atrocity.

She'd been counting the days to September 16, not because that was the day she'd been waiting for, but because she'd be able to go home, real home, bathe, sleep in a bed with Egyptian cotton sheets, and turn on the air conditioning, even if she didn't need it.

For the first time in her entire career, she missed the middle of the 21st century. She missed it with a mad passion, realizing that with all the rising sea levels, the incredible population growth, the poverty that no one could quite wipe out, the life she led there was one of privilege, even though she associated more with the upper class here than she ever had there.

Still, she stood at the door of her apartment building, and looked up at the azure sky. A perfect blue, the temperature in the low sixties, promising to be one of those spectacular New York days, the kind that made you wonder why you lived anywhere else. The city, about to enter its ascendancy in American life, glowed under the September sun.

People were walking outside and gazing upward, some even smiling, probably planning a series of errands that would get them out of the office. Folks who worked outside had smirks of superiority; they got paid to be outside.

A few people were probably thinking ahead to lunch, planning to splurge at one of the food carts, and maybe even sit on one of the benches lined up along the streets or head to one of the city's parks, if only for a few minutes. A few snatched minutes that no one would ever get.

She shuddered. She'd been in Manhattan before on a perfect September day. On one of her first jobs, in fact. She'd stood not far from here and gazed upward at a building that wasn't even a glimmer in someone's eye this morning, and watched, at 8:46 am, as American Flight 11 crashed into the World Trade Center's north tower.

The same sort of sunshine. Same kind of optimism in the air.

Only then that crisis had been more deadly, using weapons not yet dreamed of, hitting a building impossible to build in this time period, while an entire nation watched on a machine that Philo Farnsworth wouldn't even imagine for another year.

That day had been hard, but she had been prepared. She had watched the footage, read the accounts, talked to others who had also visited September 11th. And that day had been the final test in her training: could she maintain her composure as people jumped to their deaths to escape flames, as buildings pancaked around her, as first responders who wouldn't live out the day ran past her to save as many lives as possible?

She had been, in the words of her instructor, "positively

bloodless." He had meant that as a compliment, and she had taken it that way. "Positively bloodless," meant she kept her composure, did her job, and got out with a minimum of notification and a minimum of fuss.

Yes, she had nightmares. Everyone did; it was part of the job. But they weren't debilitating, and she was able to work through the worst of them with the therapist the department had assigned her.

She was, in other words, a stellar candidate, the best of her class. A woman who had since completed dozens of difficult assignments.

A woman who did not want to walk to the corner of Wall and Broad on this beautiful September morning. A woman who did not want to enter the House of Morgan to take her lowly secretary's desk with its fancy expensive Underwood typewriter, something she had been instructed to be very, very careful with because it was delicate. It wasn't delicate. The damn thing was a tank and it would take a sledgehammer to destroy it.

She would wager, if she had anyone to wager with, that the Underwood would survive today's bombing with nary a scratch.

She sighed, and stepped into the sea of humanity. Only four hours left, and she needed to make the most of them.

WASHINGTON, D.C.
MARCH 23, 2057 (SUPPOSEDLY)

ASSISTANT ATTORNEY GENERAL Preston Lane needed a moment to process the information the four people behind him had just presented.

He pivoted and faced the floor-to-ceiling window of his office in the Time Department's building. The building was known as the Bubble for a variety of reasons. The first was obvious: its round glass shape looked like a bubble. But the second was because it was protected by time bubble after time bubble after time bubble. "Time bubbles" were the nickname for "time-guards." In some ways, time bubble was more accurate, in that the bubble froze a time period into place.

He worked here instead of the Robert F. Kennedy Department of Justice building (which was a nice, but old building) because the Time Division of the Justice Department, like all time-related government departments, had offices here. The Bubble protected all who served.

The yard outside was in full spring bloom. Cherry trees lined the wall, their blossoms in full pink flower. The green grass, the emerging foliage, all spoke of a fantastic DC spring.

Which hadn't quite arrived in DC yet.

The permanent staff blew smoke up his ass about the yard. *It's enclosed, so it follows its own schedule,* the head gardener told him when he'd asked. *Think of it like a greenhouse.*

A greenhouse with a manipulated timer. He'd gone into the archives shortly after receiving his assignment and looked. This year's cherry blossoms mimicked last year's weather. Last year, the trees had reached full bloom by the end of March, just like they had for the past thirty years. This year, the trees outside the Bubble had returned to their April schedule, the one that had made this city and its cherry trees justly famous.

Plants didn't cooperate inside a time bubble. If you wanted plants to bloom and grow, they actually needed care, just like they would in a greenhouse. If you wanted to pretend that they followed the same schedule as the outside world, you didn't speed up the timeline or import different plants from different time periods. You set the yard's chronometer to its own schedule, and prayed that it worked like the rest of the world.

Which it did not. The world was/is/will always be a messy place. For the plants inside the yard, the world had an unbreakable schedule, and theoretically, the entire staff enjoyed that.

It made his skin crawl. All of this did. The deeper he got into his assignment, the more unhappy he became.

Especially with the Wall Street case.

Before he got appointed to the Time Division, someone on staff had noticed that Manhattan's financial district had been time-guarded from mid-August to mid-September 1920. Time-guards in the United States needed approval from the Time Department. The Secretary of Time had claimed she knew nothing of this, and indeed, there were no records of who or what had installed that bubble.

Plus, the bubble did not conform to government regulations.

Government-formed time bubbles existed throughout the United State's history, and they also existed now. The White House had its own time bubble, as did Congress, the Supreme Court, and the Pentagon. All of the buildings housing the Cabinet had them as well. Not every place could be protected—if someone could easily get to a United States Representative, for example, because the country did not have enough money to protect district offices. The money instead went to time-guarding polling places on each and every election day in the country, no matter how small the election.

Lane did not have the ability to reset time. Officially, no one did. But he suspected someone held that power unofficially, and that someone or those someones existed in the very government he served.

But the answer to that question was above his pay grade.

What happened to Philippa D'Arco, however, was not.

Lane took a deep breath. He'd go out into the yard and walk among the cherry blossoms if he weren't allergic to the damn things. Because he needed to move.

But he couldn't, because he had to finish this meeting. He turned his back on the windows. Wilhelmina Rutger and her three assistants still stood behind him, ignoring the comfortable chairs and the hollow tables that allowed for some selected time viewing.

His wife would be furious. He was supposed to accompany her on some important dinner for her hedge-fund business. She had probably given up on him anyway. She didn't understand the government's mandate: anyone who worked in the Bubble had to take a second oath, vowing to never ever use time travel for personal gain. Even if that gain was keeping peace in a marriage already on the rocks.

He forced his attention back to the problem at hand— not his problem, but the division's problem. They were related, after all.

"Okay, let me see if I get this straight." He had started so many conversations like this in the six months since his appointment. Time travel's complexities made his brain hurt. "D'Arco had ten windows for return and missed all of them, which is, apparently, unlike her. She's also the first investigator we've sent to the September 16th bombing who failed to return."

"Yes." Wilhelmina was petite and blond, with a friendly face completely at odds with her take-no-prisoners personality. "Philippa's body didn't return either, which is our failsafe."

Wilhelmina peered at him, as if she were testing whether or not he actually knew that. He wasn't sure he did. He tried not to look even more creeped out. He hated the way that people just vanished when they stepped into the time chamber, even if the vanishing was only for a moment or two. He didn't want to think about how he'd feel if they came back a few seconds later as a corpse.

"In other words this is extremely unusual." Lane sighed again, and swept his hand at the chairs. "Let's sit."

They did. He frowned at the assistants, having no idea who they were. Wilhelmina always seemed to bring a different set of assistants to every meeting. Lane wasn't sure if that was because she couldn't keep assistants or if her assistants swapped out due to those time complexities.

"Philippa is the first woman we've sent to the Wall Street bombing," Wilhelmina said. "Our previous investigators were all men. The first one arrived just after the time bubble burst, 12:01 pm on September 16, 1920, one minute after the bomb went off. He couldn't even get into the bomb site at Wall and Broad. We tried to have our second investigator arrive at 12:02 pm, and he couldn't do that. He could travel outside the time bubble around the financial district, but he couldn't time-travel inside it within hours of that explosion. We sent our third investigator to Manhattan one month before the explosion with the idea that he would get a job that would allow him to investigate the entire area, and see if the historical record is missing something that we should know."

Lane remembered now. "That last guy is the reason we ended up sending Philippa."

"Yes." Wilhelmina smiled, even though the smile did not go to her eyes. The smile said, *We've had this conversation and you should remember it. All of it. I hate repeating myself. Sir.*

He did remember the conversation now. He had asked her, *Why weren't we aware of the rigid class structure in New York at that time?*

It's not class structure that we're running into per se, sir, Wilhelmina had told him. *It's nepotism. To get hired in the House of Morgan, you need to have some kind of relationship with someone who does work there. And in 1920, we're at the height of the corruption that became known as the Teapot Dome Scandal. Everyone inside the New York Police Department who could hire our man won't now, because he has no ties to Tammany Hall. We—*

He'd cut her off. He had no idea what Teapot Dome was, and didn't want to find out. The same with Tammany Hall. He had some historical expertise, but it wasn't New York in the 1920s. When he accepted the President's appointment as Head of the Time Division in the Attorney General's Office, Lane had hoped to use this job to deal with interesting things, like people traveling back in time to murder someone else's grandmother who just happened to be a federal judge or something.

Instead, he was dealing with protected time periods that hadn't been protected by the proper authorities, and hints and allegations of alleged time abuse. Half his staff was somewhen else at the moment, investigating, prodding, poking, seeing there was a case. Or, as his boss, the Attorney General, liked to say when he brought potential cases to her, the staff was seeing if this was something that would "benefit us in the next election, or is it something that we can leave on the scrapheap of history for the next administration?"

Maybe he should quit, before the cynicism took him out of the game entirely.

"Sir?" Wilhelmina asked.

He'd checked out again. He wondered if he could pretend it was because he didn't understand the time paradoxes.

"No one looked at young women in that period," Wilhelmina said through gritted teeth. She was clearly repeating herself. "If they had jobs, they were clearly from the wrong class and being women, they were considered stupid."

He had no idea how anyone could find women stupid. There had to have been women like Wilhelmina in that day and age. How had anyone believed they were inferior?

"Philippa is one of our best operatives," Wilhelmina said. "She studied the bombing for three months before we sent her back. She's spent a month In Time."

Lane hated that phrase. It came from In Country, military slang for foreign territory, particularly a war zone. But its use here often confused him, because the rest of the world always wanted him to do things "in time" as well, and it meant something completely different. Like "just in the nick of time," which was the only way he'd make that dinner date now.

"Philippa couldn't have been killed in the bombing. She knew where she should stand, what she should do, where the most victims were, the greatest danger. She knew it all. She also knew she could return to us at 12:01, and give us her information. She would have come back, sir. I know it."

Wilhelmina's voice shook as she said that last, not with anger, but with sorrow. Or was it fear? Either way, he'd never heard those two emotions in her voice. Now she had his full attention.

"So what do you want to do?" he asked.

Wilhelmina was authorized to do a lot on her own. The

fact that she had come here, with a request that she hadn't yet articulated, meant something was very different.

"I want to send in an investigator, sir," Wilhelmina said.

He frowned. "We already sent in three, not counting Philippa. At a certain point, we have to decide that we have done what we can on this investigation. We only have so many resources."

"We don't leave people in the field," one of the men snapped. Everyone looked at him. He paled. "Sir. Sorry, sir. I mean, after all. She could be in trouble."

Could have been *in trouble,* Lane mentally corrected. But he didn't say it. He continued to address his questions to Wilhelmina. "Do we have information on her after September 16?"

"In a cursory search of the historical record, her alias, which is Philippa Darcy, does not show up. But it doesn't mean anything. Thirty-eight people died that day, and 143 were seriously wounded. But that was according to the statistics released long after the fact. No one put up flyers or tracked everyone who had been on the street that day. Even if they had the resources, they didn't have the will. The newspaper reports, for godssake, only listed names and address of the lower-class victims, and that was only if they got identified. The authorities didn't even know for certain if the body parts they found matched up to the—"

"I'm aware of the vagaries of the pre-technological age

of investigation," Lane said. "I'm asking if Philippa Darcy married or showed up in the public records. Maybe she had done her best to leave a message...?"

The investigators were supposed to send their recall device back if, for some odd reason, they decided to stay in the past. Only a handful of people had ever stayed, and all of those had traveled back just a few years, not more than a century.

"No message, sir," Wilhelmina said. "We checked. But Philippa is in the payroll roster in the House of Morgan for the week before. There is no payroll roster for the week of the 16th, and she isn't on it the following week."

Lane placed his hands on his knees and slid back. "Clearly there's a problem with the time-guard around that time period. What we've been doing hasn't been working, so I don't think sending another investigator into that time-guarded period is the best answer. I think you'll need to come up with a new plan to figure out how this bubble got placed, and who placed it."

One of her assistants slumped, but Wilhelmina's back straightened.

"I'm not asking for someone new to investigate the bombing or that time-guard, sir," she said in a how-dumb-are-you voice. "I'm asking to send an investigator to locate Philippa. I have to believe that she knows something, that she discovered something, and that someone is preventing her return. None of our failsafes have worked, and at least one of them should have. We should have some knowledge of what happened to her, and we have none."

"You automatically leap from this mission didn't go right to someone has harmed her?" It was Lane's turn to use the how-dumb-are-you voice. "For all we know, she could have been standing too close to the bomb when it went off, and she got vaporized. She, her device, the fail-safes, everything. After all, as you just pointed out, our information from that time period isn't exactly trustworthy. And I seem to recall that they never did figure out with any certainty what happened that day."

The third assistant grimaced. "There's a lot of evidence to suggest—"

Wilhelmina held up a hand, silencing him. "We do an out-and-back," she said. "A short mission, looking only on that day. We send in someone new. We give him the right credentials. After all, William J. Flynn took a train in from DC the moment he heard about the bombing. We can have our man take jurisdiction for just a few hours."

Lane had no idea who this William J. Flynn was, although he supposed Wilhelmina had once briefed him on that as well. So many cases, so much to remember. Maybe he would resign at the end of the year. Clearly all of these time paradoxes were taking a toll.

"I thought we already did that," Lane said. "Wasn't that our second investigator?"

She glanced at her assistants. "We had the wrong credentials."

"What?" Lane asked. He knew he hadn't heard this.

"We had legitimate New York police department credentials, but we had given our man a position too high up in the department. They figured out fairly quickly that he was a fraud. Only they figured he worked for former Commissioner Arthur Woods, not that he had come from the future."

Arthur Woods. Another name Lane probably should have remembered. He sighed. He would have to read up on this entire investigation just to refresh his memory. He could either do that, or trust the woman who sat before him.

"How much will this cost the department?" Lane asked.

"It depends," she said flatly. "You can calculate the loss of a human life and the loss of the training we invested into the investigator, or you can figure the price of one more trip into time."

"Possibly losing another investigator," he said.

"Possibly," she said.

"If we do, we both lose our jobs," he said.

"*That's* what's worrying you?" she asked.

"No," he said. "It isn't. What worries me is that we're doing something we don't entirely understand. We're throwing more resources at it rather than investigating the best methods and then taking them. There is no hurry, Ms. Rutger, as you've often told me. If we send in someone today or next week, it won't matter. They'll still go back to the same time period."

She raised her chin ever so slightly. He had gotten through.

"You're right, of course," she said. "In my concern, I had forgotten that. We will conduct a more thorough investigation, and then I will consult with you again."

"Thank you," he said.

Wilhelmina and her assistants left, but he remained seated. Something about this disturbed him greatly. Not Wilhelmina's hurry or even the assistants' passion. In fact, he understood the assistants' passion. They could have been the ones on the front lines. But for the luck of the draw, this conversation could have been about any one of them.

No, something else bothered Lane.

New York's financial district. Three major attacks that he knew of: this one in 1920, the 1993 bombing of the World Trade Center, and the 2001 destruction of the World Trade Center. Plus at least two thwarted attacks, one in 2012 against the Federal Reserve in lower Manhattan, and another in 2025 against the New York Stock Exchange.

Were they all time-guarded events? If so, were they time-guarded by Homeland or Justice or the Time Department? Or by someone else? Something else? A multinational? A foreign government?

Lane stood up slowly. He had to make a choice here. He could remain the ignorant figurehead, disappointed in the job that they had given him, or he could step into his role as the chief investigator of time irregularities for the Federal Government.

He hated those dinners his wife planned. He used to love investigative work. He'd simply been overwhelmed by his learning curve and, if he were honest, by the fact that he walked through several time bubbles every morning when he came to work. He hated the Bubble, but everywhere he'd worked in DC had a time-guard of one type or another. The problem wasn't the job; the problem was his attitude.

He'd allowed others to dictate policy during his first six months here. Time to change that, no pun intended. Or maybe he did intend to pun. Because it was past time. And he couldn't use the amazing resources at his disposal to start again. So maybe he could use them to solve something huge.

Or, if this wasn't huge, just to make the right decision in the Philippa D'Arcy case.

Whatever that decision might be.

MANHATTAN

SEPTEMBER 16, 1920

P HILIPPA GLANCED AT the clock hanging on the far wall. The incredible clack of typewriters had its own rhythm, a *rat-a-tat-tat-tat-tat-tat-tat-tat bing!* that had become familiar to her. At the desk next to her, the new hire sang "Over There" faintly under her breath, a reprieve from the Tin Pan Alley tunes she had started the morning with. The last few hours of Philippa's last day. She looked at all the girls around her, intent on their typing or fixing their shorthand or stacking already-completed letters in manila folders, and wondered how they would fare.

They might be all right. The large room had no windows, the grillwork making it seem like a prison. All of the girls who worked there wore white shirtwaists and long skirts, their hair in a neat bun. They seemed interchangeable and probably were, to the men who ran the House of Morgan.

Philippa straightened her desk, rolled a sheet of House of Morgan letterhead in the platen of her Underwood, and stood up.

Mrs. Fontaine looked up from her desk. It faced the rows and rows of desks.

"You do not have permission to stand," she said. She was twice the age of the girls and twice their weight. She ran a tight office, but a fair one. She pretended to be an ogre, but the girls loved her, because she understood what it was to be young and employed and a little bit terrified.

"I'm sorry," Philippa said. "I'm afraid I need a personal moment."

Technically, the girls weren't to leave their desks until their thirty minute unpaid lunch break. But Mrs. Fontaine understood that women couldn't always sit that long, particularly at certain times of the month. She claimed she got her girls to do five times the work the girls in other financial houses did, because she allowed them "personal moments."

Mrs. Fontaine nodded. "Make it quick."

Philippa wouldn't make it quick. Not that it mattered. After noon today, she would no longer be employed at the House of Morgan.

She would make one more tour around the building, and try to see if there was something unusual. Then she would return to her desk and prevent some of the girls whom she'd befriended from taking their usual lunch. They would be safe inside their windowless room, but on that street, near the Curb Market, the Sub-Treasury, the New York Stock Exchange annex, and all of the other buildings, people would die, lose limbs, have their lives forever changed.

Technically, she wasn't supposed to prevent that. Technically, she was supposed to go about her business. But there was no way of knowing what the girls would have done without her, so trying to play that game didn't work. She had to live with herself, and even though, in her real life, in her real time, these women were long dead, they were alive now, she'd been their friend, and she owed them.

She slipped a steno pad into the pocket of her long skirt, and stepped away from her desk. She smiled a thank you to Mrs. Fontaine, then headed in the direction of the women's necessary. The one great thing about the House of Morgan was that it had bathrooms and they were clean. Not that she needed to use one.

She waited until she was out of Mrs. Fontaine's sight, then pulled the steno pad from the pocket of her skirt. She hugged the pad against her chest and then wandered, making certain she looked lost.

It had worked every time she had done this in the past. Some man would ask her where she needed to go, she would give an answer, and he would point her in the right direction. The younger men would ask her name, and give her a bright smile. The older men would sometimes put their arm around her and guide her to the correct floor.

She didn't want either to happen today. She needed to do her last tour unescorted. Then, if she didn't find anything, she would slip onto the street and run to the Sub-Treasury building.

She couldn't get their mission off her mind either. Right now, as she patrolled the inside of the House of Morgan, workers at the Sub-Treasury building were transferring a billion dollars in gold coins and bullion to the federal assay office across the street.

She had no real idea how they were doing this; her reading told her that the workers were using a wooden chute, and after the bombing, a U.S. Army battalion would arrive to protect the gold.

Initially the Time Crimes Division believed someone was trying to steal the gold. After the first investigator discovered that no gold got stolen, someone suggested that the time-guard had been put into place to *prevent* the gold from getting stolen, and had been successful.

But that didn't make sense either, because the gold would be a lot easier to steal after the bombing than before. Hell, she could figure out how to do it: she could time travel into the Sub-Treasury or next to the chute in the assay office at 12:01 in the chaos. With the right kind of manpower and weaponry, the gold would disappear.

But it didn't; it wouldn't; it never would. It would remain.

The fact that she was even thinking of heading to the Sub-Treasury building showed just how desperate she was to get some information, any information, before she left 1920 at 12:02 pm. She had already been to Sub-Treasury courtesy of a nice young guard, who had thought her harmless. A different nice young guard had shown her what he could in the assay office, and there, she found nothing out of the ordinary.

Not that she knew what she was looking for. Something. Something had to be here, besides this bombing.

Something had to be so important that changing it threatened The Way Things Were.

She walked up a marble staircase to the private meetings floor. She'd been called into a few of these conference rooms. She'd sat on a wooden chair in the back and taken notes.

Today, if someone asked where she was going, she had a half-plausible lie based on that previous experience. She knew that Junius Spencer Morgan the younger, the heir to the throne, was having a meeting in one of the rooms facing Wall Street. She'd seen photographs of the aftermath, although she wasn't sure which room he was in. If someone stopped her, she would tell them she was going to relieve the secretary handling that meeting.

But no one stopped her. She went up staircase after staircase to floor after floor and she was about to give up, when she noticed one of the doors to the maintenance area stood open.

She'd tried that door in the past, and it had been locked. This time, she slipped inside.

Four men were leaning together, gesturing and whispering. They appeared to be arguing. They didn't notice her.

They didn't look like maintenance men. They were too clean for one thing. People who did physical labor in this decade had a layer of grime on their clothes and skin that just couldn't come off in a weekly bath. Their clothes were off too. A little too shiny, a bit too new. And one man wore shoes that had a metal ridge she had never seen before. Or, rather, that she hadn't seen in a very long time. Or, rather, that no one would see for many many years.

The men all looked at her at the same time. One man flushed red.

"Can we help you?" asked the man wearing the odd shoes. He had dark eyes and skin that wasn't quite white. She wouldn't have noticed that a month ago, but after living here, in a world where everything was defined by skin color, last name, education, and accent, she noticed.

Her heart started pounding. Her planned lie about Mr. Morgan seemed wrong, somehow.

"I saw the open door..." she said.

"Christ," hissed the man who flushed. "She saw us. No one was supposed to see us."

His teeth were white. Even. Perfect. So were the teeth of the first man who spoke. So were her teeth. People here remarked on that.

These men didn't belong here any more than she did. And, she would wager, no one in the Time Division knew about them.

She backed out of the room, slammed the door closed, and ran for the stairs. With one hand, she lifted her skirt enough so that her own boots didn't catch, and with the other, she put the steno pad in her pocket. Then she reached for the railing. The steps were slick, and she had to slow down some.

She heard footsteps behind her. She sped up just as someone grabbed her. He smelled of cologne. Not Bay Rum. Cologne. Nothing from this time period. It was too subtle, too complex. And the hand that covered her mouth had had a manicure.

She bit his palm. He cursed, but didn't let her go. Instead, he dragged her up the stairs. She struggled, but couldn't free herself. Her feet banged on every step, jarring her all the way up her spine.

Surely, someone on the lower levels heard that. Surely,

someone would come investigate. Surely, someone would do something.

She elbowed the man, then tried to hit his face with her fists. When he pulled her onto the upper floor, she levered herself up on his arm and kicked him on his shins. He didn't even flinch. He continued to drag her. One of the other men joined him, and they flung her into that room.

She slid along the floor on her skirt, and nearly slammed into the wall. The men peered down at her.

"What do we do with her?" asked the man who had flushed.

The man who had dragged her reached down, and pulled her lips back so that he could look at her teeth like she was a horse. She tried to bite him again.

"Feisty bit of business," one of the other men said.

"Who are you, really?" the man who dragged her asked.

"Philippa Darcy," she snapped, using the name she used in this period. "I'm expected in Mr. Morgan's office."

"It's eleven-thirty," one of the men said to the others.

The man who dragged her grinned. "Then I'll wager that Mr. Morgan won't mind if you don't show up. He probably won't even notice."

"He *will*," she said, keeping to the game. "He'll notice. He'll send someone searching for me."

"Nice try, honey," said the man who dragged her. "But you girls aren't that important to anyone in the House of Morgan. No one except your boss even knows your name."

"What do we do with her?" the man who flushed asked again.

"We can't send her home for another 31 minutes," said the man with the shoes.

Her heart rate increased. They knew. They knew about the bomb; they probably knew that she didn't belong here.

"What's really going on?" she asked.

"Ah, honey," said the man who dragged her. "That's above your pay grade. It's strictly need-to-know."

She struggled to her feet. Damn the skirt. Her legs caught in its folds.

"I think I need to know," she said, with more bravado than she felt.

"And you will know," the man who dragged her said. Then he grinned. "All in good time."

And all of the men laughed, as if he had told a particularly witty joke.

WASHINGTON, D.C.
MARCH 23, 2057 (SUPPOSEDLY)

LANE WAS DEEP in his research when his assistant peeked her head in the door. He nearly snapped at her, but thought the better of it. Her lips were in a thin line, her hair slightly out of place. She looked frazzled, and one reason he had hired her was because she was the most unflappable person he had ever met.

"The Attorney General just called a meeting downstairs," she said. "He says it's urgent."

"I thought nothing was urgent in the Time Division," Lane said.

"Apparently," she said, "this is."

MANHATTAN

SEPTEMBER 16, 1920

AT 11:55 AM, Charles Gage took his seat at the back of Fred Eberlin's New Street restaurant. The place smelled of frying meat and spilled beer. The table was sticky, and even in the middle of the day, the electric lights were on. They weren't very powerful, and they barely cut the gloom.

The waiter who had greeted him didn't want him to sit so far back.

"Wouldn't you rather have a seat up front by the window, sir?" he asked as Gage strode toward the back of the restaurant. "You can watch all of New York go by without moving a muscle."

"Not today," Gage said. Today, if he sat by that plate glass window, or any plate glass window within six blocks of Wall Street, he ran the risk of serious injury, maybe even death.

Even sitting this far back was a risk. But he wanted to be inside the time-guard. Within the hour, the police would block off sections of Wall Street, and he wouldn't be able to get in unless his paperwork was perfect.

He didn't want to rely on perfect paperwork. He wanted to rely on outsmarting whatever it was that had set up the time bubble in the first place.

The waiter sighed loudly. "The specials are on the board up front, sir, but I suppose I can recite them for you."

"I'd rather have a sarsaparilla," Gage said. He'd acquired a taste for the damn things on another job, ten years ago his time, but only a year before this one. He had a hunch that whatever the Coca-Cola company used to make the drink was bad for him, but he didn't care. It was a taste he couldn't get anywhere else. If, of course, he had time to drink it.

He pulled out his pocket watch. He'd set it to New York time the moment he arrived. He couldn't get to Washington D.C. on September 16, so he'd had to settle for Philadelphia which, for some reason, wasn't time-guarded at all. He took a train to Manhattan, and arrived at Penn Station at nine a.m. Then he'd walked down the island, and stopped near the Equitable Life Insurance Building, which, at 38 stories, was currently the tallest building in the city, if not the world.

He'd loitered outside for as long as he could, watching the cutthroat operatives of the outdoor Curb Market trade the junk stocks and bonds that the regular markets sneered at. Part of him was fascinated to see history in action. The Curb Market's annex was nearly finished, and these traders would move inside within the year. But for the moment, they acted like street vendors, waving their tickets and shouting to be heard.

But he couldn't simply observe them. He needed to keep an eye on the street. He was watching for a touring car with a New Jersey license plate. He was also looking for some sort of old wooden wagon being pulled by an elderly horse. The horse would end up in pieces all over Wall Street, as would the wagon. The touring car would end up on its side.

Smart money believed that the car rear-ended the wagon, which had probably come from the DuPont Powder Works with a load of dynamite. Manhattan had banned the transport of explosives on its streets during the daylight hours, but that didn't mean that companies followed the rules.

He saw the touring car, recognizing its plate—NJ24246—and realized that the man who claimed to be the chauffer in the news reports looked nothing like the man driving. Then Gage saw a brand new wagon being pulled by an elderly horse. He wished he could take video, but he didn't dare. He was already attracting enough attention by standing outside the Equitable Building.

He'd slipped through the crowds and made his way to the restaurant where he sat now, wondering if the things he had seen had any meaning whatsoever.

Not that he was here for the bombing. He wasn't. He was here to find Philippa D'Arco, or Darcy as they called her. Her image was stamped—literally—inside his mind. One of those chips that the investigators for the Justice Department used on occasion. He knew what she looked like when she walked, talked, laughed, as if he had known her well. He wouldn't be able to miss her any more than a lover or her own family would have.

If Gage saw her. If he found her.

He wasn't entirely sure she was still here. He had telephoned the House of Morgan that morning, and asked if she was working. He'd been told that secretaries did not receive personal calls while at work, and then someone had asked his name.

"I'm her father," he had lied. "Her mother's gravely ill. I would like to speak to her."

"You may do so during her regular luncheon," the young man who had answered the phone told him. "All female secretaries take luncheon beginning at noon."

"But she is in the office?" Gage pressed.

"She signed in at 7:45 am, sir. Good day." And the young man had hung up.

So Gage had three pieces of information to take back with him. Philippa D'Arcy had shown up to work. The chauffer on the touring car did not look like his photograph in the papers from the hearings. And the wagon that might or might not have been carrying the dynamite was brand new.

The waiter set down a tall glass with the greenish brown liquid foaming inside. Gage picked it up, hoping for one sip before all hell broke loose—

And then the world went white. A sound, louder than anything he'd ever heard, shook the building. The air turned fire hot, then evaporated, and his lungs ached. He dove under the table. Too late. Already shards of glass had slid their way here.

Everything went deadly quiet. Nothing. Not a single sound. Almost as if all of New York held its breath at the same moment.

And then someone moaned.

The waiter was crouched against the back wall. The two customers who had been sitting near the window were sprawled on the floor. Another waiter leaned against the counter, still clutching a plate of food.

Gage stood, ran his hands over his suit, checking to see if he was uninjured. He was. He knocked some glass shards out of his hair, picked up his hat, and shook it off as well.

The screams were beginning, as were the cries for help.

He took a deep breath, tasting smoke, blood, and something acrid, but at least there was oxygen again. He steeled his shoulders, and stepped into what he knew would be the hardest few minutes of his life.

He had to step over the injured, pass the dumbstruck, avoid the helpless, and head for the door. It had been blown open by the force of the explosion. A young man sprawled on the steps, bleeding from a gash in the head. His trembling right hand reached for a spiked rail that had ripped through the shoulder of his suit.

That had to be George Lacina, who worked at Equitable Life Assurance, the man whose comment to *The New York World* had set off all sorts of alarms in 2057. Lacina said that he later noticed that all the buttons on his coat had come off, and his watch was ten minutes slow.

Almost as if time had stopped. Or gone backward. Or rippled.

All signs of a time-guard.

Gage glanced at his pocket watch. It appeared to have stopped. But as he looked at it, the second hand moved. He needed to do the same.

It was easier said than done. Hundreds of people poured out of buildings, hurried down stairs, and ran away from the financial district. Some of them bleeding, many of them covered in glass or plaster, all of them looking terrified.

He had to go upstream, pushing through them all, careful not to fall or he would be trampled to death. All the while his feet slipped on blood or severed limbs or body parts he couldn't identify.

A woman on fire screamed as she ran past him. A man tackled her from the side, wrapping her in a coat.

Gage pretended he didn't see, reminded himself it was history. When that didn't work, he lied to himself that it was a virtual simulation—and he'd been through hundreds of those. Thousands. He couldn't help these people. They were more than a century dead, and for most, this was the worst day of their lives. But he couldn't reach out, couldn't do anything.

He had to find Philippa.

He reached the House of Morgan, pushed his way up the narrow steps toward the open doors. People still poured out, but he didn't see her among them. He caught some of the women who looked unhurt.

"Philippa," he said. "Where's Philippa?"

Mostly they shook their heads, then shook him off. One heavyset older woman frowned at him, said, "She went ... necessary. But ... an hour ago."

Only she was gone before he could parse out what that meant. Or what he hoped it had meant. Philippa had gone to the ladies room an hour before and had never come back.

If she was a smart little time traveler, she would have vanished by now, safe back in 2057, inside the Bubble, making her report. But he was here because she hadn't done that. Her body hadn't shown up, her chip hadn't activated, her failsafe device hadn't returned.

He knew his chip would survive a blast—he'd been through half a dozen of them, not to mention the fact that everything was tested for all kinds of conditions—so he doubted her equipment had failed.

He kept grabbing people, asking, "Philippa?" and getting no response.

Except from a red-haired young man, wearing shirt-sleeves, and ripped pants.

"Thought I saw her upstairs," he said, voice trembling. "Lordy, I hope she's all right."

Gage nodded, kept moving, found the stairs, tried to ignore what he saw. Couldn't ignore all of it. The young man held into place by something large—a bit of wall, maybe?—pinning his skull to his teller cage. The man with the broken leg trying to help another man bleeding from the face. The woman ripping pieces of her skirt and using them to tie off oozing wounds.

Above the trading floor, the glass dome that marked this part of the House of Morgan creaked. People screamed and dove for the walls. He didn't. He knew it wouldn't collapse.

Junius Morgan, carrying a wounded man toward the door. His face was scorched, his clothing blood-covered, but he seemed determined.

All of these people were heroes. Gage wasn't. He couldn't be. He had to keep searching for Philippa.

He explored several floors, saw more wounded, but no more dead, avoided some of the dazed victims, and kept searching. He didn't see her and no one seemed to know where she was.

He spent nearly two hours inside the House of Morgan, exploring each room, seeing all the damage—which was much more considerable than the papers ever made it out to be—and he found no trace of her.

It was as if she had followed instructions and vanished. Only she hadn't.

Finally, when he walked out of the bank, exhausted and covered in dirt and blood, he braced himself. Time to assume his identity as a Pinkerton, pretending he'd been hired by the Equitable Company, since the House of Morgan was unofficially using William J. Burns's International Detective Agency.

He would find Philippa, or the parts of her, or what became of her, if he had to stay here for the next year to do so.

WASHINGTON, D.C.
MARCH 23, 2057 (SUPPOSEDLY)

THE CONFERENCE ROOM, bunkered under the building, was an unassuming little space, modeled on the White House's Situation Room. Bunkered, time-guarded with all the latest gadgetry, but so shielded that no one could travel in even from inside the Bubble itself.

Lane hated the little room. It looked like something out of time itself. Rectangular, with blond wood paneling, matching table, and the most uncomfortable blue chairs in the world, the room was always stuffy and tension-filled.

He was the last person to arrive, and as he pulled the door open, he had only seconds to prepare. No one had warned him that he faced not only the Attorney General, but Cabinet Secretaries from Treasury and Time as well.

And, off in a corner, as if he were monitoring the meeting instead of participating in it, Brandon Carnelius, the Chairman of the Federal Reserve.

Lane had barely gotten the door closed when the Attorney General said, "You need to recall Charles Gage from 1920."

Kayla Huntingdon was not known for her diplomatic skills, something that had gotten her into trouble with Congress more than once. Sometimes Lane wondered how she ever made it through her confirmation.

"We lost an operative," Lane said. "And we've found some anomalies."

"We know," said Noah Singh. He ran Treasury. He *was* known for his diplomacy, not that it showed at the moment. "Recall him anyway."

Lane knew better than to remind Singh that he did not work for Treasury. Annabelle Tsu, the Time Secretary, nodded. "We have decided. We're going to leave the time-guard in place."

"We didn't create it," Lane said. "I've researched. It didn't come from the government."

"Not technically," Singh said. "But you needn't worry about it."

Lane looked at Huntingdon. He realized from the set of her full mouth that she was furious. She had not been informed about something. Tsu's long red fingernails tapped on the tabletop. Apparently she hadn't been informed either.

"You want to tell me what's going on?" Lane asked. He'd directed the question at his boss, Huntingdon, but he didn't care who answered.

"Technically, you don't have the security clearance," Singh said. "We've decided to bring you into this, since you might run into an anomaly, as you call it, again, and we need you to be prepared."

Huntingdon looked down, her blond hair covering her face. Lane had seen her do that before. It was a deliberate move so that no one could see her expression. Yep, she was pissed. And he had a hunch he was about to be.

"I'm not sure that you're aware of the fact that the Federal Reserve System was founded in 1913," Singh said.

"I know my history," Lane said.

"Let him speak," Tsu said quietly.

"And worked with other central bankers in other nations during the various wars. The Fed's powers expanded after the Great Depression, the Great Recession, and of course, the recent Currency Crisis," Singh said. He sounded like every bad professor Lane had ever had.

"Let me cut through the bullshit for you," Huntingdon said. "Somewhere along the way, these so-called financial geniuses figured the only way to control monetary policy was to change it. By going backwards."

"What?" Lane blinked. No one was supposed to alter

major historical events just because they hadn't worked properly. Or what this generation thought of as properly. "They can't do that. It's not legal."

"We started our policy before it was illegal," Carnelius intoned from his corner. As if that made it right. There were laws in place to cover such things. Otherwise someone could go back in time and do something that wasn't a crime then, but was now, and be completely immune from prosecution.

Lane started to say that, but Tsu shook her head. Tsu, who looked as angry as Huntingdon.

"Forgive me, sir," Lane said to the Fed Chair, knowing he was out of turn. "But we're all forbidden from messing with Time."

"Yes, we are" Singh said, taking the focus off Carnelius. "The Fed knows that now. But they started before the rest of us. Interestingly enough, they had time travel devices long before anyone else did. And they did things that they've been trying to clean up ever since. You're probably most familiar with the Flash Crash of 2010? That was an error on the part of the time travelers from the International Monetary Fund, who are tied into this as well."

"I don't understand," Lane said.

"Someone," Huntingdon said, "and no one will say who..." and with that she looked at Carnelius, "tried to use a time device in 1920. And then tried to cover it up. Which is why all the original detectives from the Bureau of Investigation to the New York Police Department to the private detectives had no real idea what happened, because *all* of their theories were true."

Lane got cold. A messy cover-up led to conflicting time stories, which led to bad investigations, which lead to chaos that often cost lives. Like it had in this instance.

"We cannot investigate the so-called bombing without making matters worse," Huntingdon said. "So call off your people. And when you hit a similar time-guarded moment related to something financial, check before you send investigators into the past."

"Wouldn't it be easier if we knew what periods to avoid?" Lane asked Huntingdon.

Her lower jaw moved slightly before she responded. "It would. And yet, apparently, the Fed is not in the business of making our lives easier."

Carnelius shook his head slightly, as if no one understood him.

Lane filtered several responses before he said the one thing he felt he had the right to say, "We've been working on the Wall Street Bombing for nearly a year of our time. We've used a lot of resources. Why has this just come up now?"

"Because," Carnelius said, "one of your operatives stumbled on some of ours."

"Who?" Lane asked. "And when?"

"In 1920. Miss Philippa—Darcy? D'Arco? She stumbled on my people. The moment they found out who she was, they sent word to us."

Time didn't work that way, but the language didn't keep up. They'd found out in 1920, but when had they discovered it in 2057? Or had they? How had word gotten back? Lane didn't know, and he had a hunch everyone would say he didn't have the right to ask.

"When can we get her back?" he asked. That at least, would be a victory. He wouldn't have lost an investigator to this ridiculous operation.

"They won't give her back," Huntingdon said, the frustration clear in her voice.

"See here, Kayla. It's not quite like that," Singh said.

"She can't come back," Tsu said. "She knows too much."

"She's ours now," Carnelius said. "You don't need to worry about her. We'll take good care of her."

"Like you took good care of Wall Street in 1920?" Lane snapped.

"Prescott," Singh said. "Some respect."

"Yes, respect would've been nice, wouldn't it?" Lane said as he got up. "Thirty-eight dead, hundreds more injured, in what history considers the worst act of terrorism on American soil until a bombing in Oklahoma City in 1995? All caused by some idiots mishandling time travel for the Federal Reserve."

"Technically, it wasn't us," Carnelius said. "We're not the only Central Bank with time travel capabilities."

"Oh, that makes it so much better." Lane spread his hands on the tabletop and looked at Huntingdon. "I'm going to tender my resignation."

"And I'll have to refuse it," she said. "With this kind of secret, you have just become a lifer in the Time Division."

Lane's breath caught. He felt a moment of terror that he then suppressed. "You can't do that. I serve at the whim of the President."

"And at whose whim does the President serve?" Tsu muttered.

"Enough," Singh said. "This meeting is over. And it never happened."

"Of course not." Lane felt dizzy. "Just like I never lost an investigator."

"You didn't lose her," Carnelius said. "You simply transferred her to a better paying job."

"I did nothing of the sort," Lane said. "I want that on the record."

"What record?" Huntingdon asked. "This meeting never happened."

Lane tilted his head back. His brain hurt. And this wasn't even a time paradox. It was a political one, with real repercussions on real people's lives.

"When will you return her to us?" he asked.

"We won't," Carnelius said. "She's ours now. Forever."

That would have sounded ominous outside of the Bubble. Inside it, it was damn near terrifying.

"I suppose you won't tell me what that means," Lane said.

"It means she's elsewhen." Carnelius stood. "And that's all I'm going to say."

MANHATTAN
SEPTEMBER 1, 2088 (SUPPOSEDLY)

"YOU'VE GOT TO be kidding," Philippa said. She sat on what looked like air, a clear chair that was more comfortable than anything she felt in weeks. "I have to stay here?"

"Not here, exactly," said the man who had dragged her. His name was Roland Karinki, and he worked for the Time Unit in the Federal Reserve. At the moment, they were in the Manhattan Fed, in a room that literally vanished in the clouds. "You're free to leave this job, to do whatever you want."

"But I can't go home," she said.

"If by that you mean 2057, no, you cannot. It's forbidden to you now. But we can use your services here or in the distant past. We have a lot to do."

She tried not to look panicked. She tried not to *be*

49

panicked. Her training had warned her that she might get stuck out of her time. It wasn't supposed to bother her. She was positively bloodless, after all.

But she didn't feel bloodless.

"I liked 2057," she said. "No, I loved 2057."

"I believe you," Karinki said. "At least you're not trying to lie to me by saying that you're leaving behind friends and family. I know Time Division forbids both of those."

"Not friends," she said, although if she were being truthful, she had not been encouraged to have good friends.

Which made her wonder about all those girls she'd worked with in the House of Morgan. Had they made it out safely? Were they badly wounded? Would she ever know?

"You'll like it better here," Karinki said. "I promise."

"Promises from a man who grabbed me and tossed me into a room, then took me out of my life. Great. How do I know I can trust you?"

"Because," he said. "I have orders from your boss. Do you recall Prescott Lane? He left a file for you, which you can view at your leisure."

She narrowed her gaze. "I know nothing about 2088. You could have faked it."

"I could have," Karinki said. "But I didn't. *We* didn't. And we will help you adjust."

She leaned her head back, and thought for a moment. She was somewhen else. That was what she wanted when she woke up this morning in that wretched two-room flat, with two smelly girls beside her on a flea-ridden mattress. And she had a hunch the food would be better than it had been in 1920. The attitudes would be better as well. And then there was the matter of comfort.

Maybe she was positively bloodless. Because she could feel herself transitioning to the new when.

"I need a hot shower," she said. "Some new clothes. And a bed in a place that has climate control."

"That's easy," Karinki said. "How about dinner?"

"Sure," she said. "Alone. In my new apartment. With all kinds of information at my fingertips about the last thirty-one years. I won't make a decision until I know what my options are."

"Fair enough," he said, and then extended his hand. "Welcome to the future."

She looked at his palm. It was clean, but it had bite marks on the fleshy part that he hadn't yet cleaned up.

"It sure as hell better be nicer than the past," she said.

"Time periods are never one thing," he said. "You should know that."

She did know it. Maybe better than he did.

Maybe better than anyone.

She looked out that window at Lower Manhattan. Sunlight reflected off the Equitable Building struggling to survive between skyscrapers she couldn't identify. Through the buildings' canyons, she saw the Upper Bay, Battery

Park, and a clean Statue of Liberty. Saw New Jersey in the distance.

"What month is it?" she asked.

He grinned. "September."

She looked outside again, but not down this time. Up, like people on the sidewalks in 1920. She saw a clear blue September sky. The kind that promised one of those spectacular New York days, the kind that made you wonder why you lived anywhere else.

"I'm staying in Manhattan," she said. "I don't care when. But I do care where."

He studied her for a moment, then nodded. "We can arrange that."

"Good," she said. "Because I wouldn't work for you any other way."

YOU MIGHT LIKE THIS...

THE END OF THE WORLD

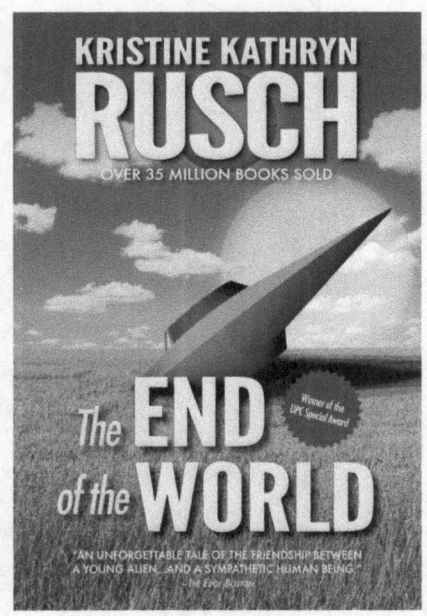

THEN

The air reeked of smoke.

The people ran, and the others chased them.

She kept tripping. Momma pulled her forward, but Momma's hand was slippery. Her hand slid out, and she fell, sprawling on the wooden sidewalk.

Momma reached for her, but the crowd swept Momma forward.

All she saw was Momma's face, panicked, her hands, grasping, and then Momma was gone.

Everyone ran around her, over her, on her. She put her hands over her head and cringed, curling herself into a little ball.

She made herself change color. Brown-gray like the sidewalk, with black lines running up and down.

Dress hems skimmed over her. Boots brushed her. Heels pinched the skin on her arms.

No spikes, Momma always said. *No spikes or they'll know.*

So she held her breath, hoping the spikes wouldn't break through her skin because she was so scared, and her side hurt where someone's boot hit it, and the wooden sidewalk bounced as more and more people ran past her.

Finally, she started squinching, like Daddy taught her before he left.

Slide, he said. *A little bit at a time. Slide. Squinch onto whatever surface you're on and cling.*

It was hard to squinch without spikes, but she did, her head tucked in her belly, her hair trailing to one side. More boots stomped on it, pulling it, but she bit her lower lip so that she wouldn't have to think about the pain.

She was almost to the bank door when the sidewalk stopped shaking. No one ran by her. She was alone.

She flattened herself against the brick and shuddered. Her skin smelled of chewing tobacco, spit and beer from the saloon next door.

She had shut down her ears, but she finally rotated them outward. Men were shouting, women yelling. There was pounding and screaming and a high-pitched noise she didn't like.

If they found her flattened against the brick, they'd know. If they saw the spikes rise from her body, they'd know. If they saw her squinching, they'd know.

But she couldn't move.

She was shivering, and she didn't know what to do.

NOW

The call didn't come through channels. It rang to Becca Keller's personal cell.

Chase Waterston hadn't even said hello.

"Got a problem at the End of the World," he'd said, his usually self-assured voice shaky. "Can you get here right away? Just you."

Normally, she would have told him to call the precinct or 911, but something stopped her. Probably that scared edge to his voice, a sound she'd never heard in all the years she'd known him.

She drove from the center of downtown Hope to the End of the World, a drive that, in the old days, would have taken five minutes. Now it took twenty, and the only thing that kept her from being annoyed at the traffic were the mountains, bleak and cold, rising up like goddesses at the edge of Hope.

Hope was a mountain city, but its terrain was high desert. Vast expanses of brown still marked the outskirts of town, although the interior had lost much of its desert feel. By the time she passed the latest ticky-tacky development, she hit the rolling dunes of her childhood. Even though she had on the air-conditioning, the smell of sagebrush blew in —full of promise.

If she kept going straight too much farther, she'd hit small windy roads filled with switchbacks that led to now-trendy ski resorts. If she turned right, she'd follow the old stage coach route over the edge of the mountains into the Willamette Valley where most of Oregon's population lived.

The End of the World was an ancient resort at the fork between the mountain roads and the old stagecoach route. At the turn of the previous century, some enterprising entrepreneur figured travelers who were taking the narrow road toward the Willamette Valley would welcome a place to rest and recover from the long dusty trip.

Now bumper-to-bumper traffic filled that wagon route, which had expanded to a four-lane highway. Hope actually had a real rush hour, thanks to ex-patriate Californians, retired baby boomers, and ridiculously cheap housing.

Chase was rebuilding the resort for those baby boomers and Californians. For some reason, he thought they'd want to stay in a hundred-year-old hotel, with a view of the mountains and the river, even in the heat of the summer and the deep cold of the desert winter.

Becca steered the squad with her left hand and fiddled with the air-conditioner with her right, wishing her own car was out of the shop. No matter what she did, she couldn't get the squad car cooled. Nothing seemed to be working properly. Or maybe that was the effect of the heat.

It was a hundred and three degrees, and the third week without rain. The radio's most recent weather report promised the temperature would reach one hundred and eight by the time the day was over.

Finally, she reached the construction site.

Chase had set up the site so that it only blocked part of the ever-present wind and as a consequence, the dust billowed across the highway with the gusts.

The city had cited Chase twice for the hazard, and he'd promised to fix it just after the Fourth of July holiday. It looked like he'd been keeping his word, too. A huge plastic construction fence leaned against the old building. Graders and post-diggers were parked on the side of the road.

Nothing moved. Not the cats Chase had been using to dig out the old parking lot, not the crane he'd rented the week before, and not the crew, most of whom sat on the backs of pick-up trucks, their faces blackened with dust and grime and too much sun. She could see their eyes, white against the darkness of their skins, watching her as she turned onto the dirt path that Chase had been using as an access road.

He was waiting for her in the doorway of what had once been a natatorium. Built over an old underground spring, the Natatorium had once boasted the largest swimming pool in Eastern Oregon. There was some kind of pipe system which pumped water into the pool, keeping it perpetually cold. In the Natatorium's heyday, the water had been replaced daily.

Behind the Natatorium was the old five-story brick hotel that still had the original fixtures. No vandals had ever attacked the place. Even the windows were intact.

Becca had gone inside more than once, first as an impressionable twelve-year-old, and ever since, part of her believed the rumors that the hotel was haunted.

She pulled up beside the Natatorium door, in a tiny patch of shade provided by the overhanging roof. She got out and the blast-furnace heat hit her, prickling sweat on her skin almost instantly. Apparently the air conditioner had been working in the piece-of-crap squad after all.

Chase watched her. His lips were chapped, his skin fried blackish red from the sun. He had weather-wrinkles around his eyes and narrow mouth. His hair was cropped short, and over it he wore a regulation hardhat. He clutched another one in his left hand, slapping it rhythmically against his thigh.

"Thanks for coming, Becca," he said, and he still sounded shaken.

The tone was unfamiliar, but the expression on his face wasn't. She'd seen it only once, after she'd told him she wanted out, that his values and hers were so different, she couldn't stomach a relationship any longer.

"What do you got, Chase?" she asked.

"Come with me." He handed her the hardhat he'd been holding.

She took it as a gust of wind caught her short hair and blew its clipped edges into her face. She slipped the hardhat on, and tucked her hair underneath it, then followed Chase inside the building.

It was hotter inside the Natatorium, and the air smelled of rot and mold. She usually thought of those as humidity smells, but the Natatorium's interior was so dry that it was crumbly.

The floor was shredded with age, the wood so brittle that she wondered if it would hold her weight. Most of the walls were gone, the remains of them piled in a corner. Chase had gutted the interior.

When she had been a girl, she had played in this place. Her parents had forbidden her to come, which made it all the more inviting. The rot and mold smells had been present even then. But the walls had still been up, and there had been some ancient furniture in here as well, made unusable by weather and critters chewing the interior.

She used to stand inside the entrance with the door open, the stream of sunlight carrying a spinning tunnel of dust motes. When she closed her eyes halfway, she could just imagine the people arriving here after a long day of travel, happy to be in a place of such elegance, such warmth.

But now even that sense of a long ago but lively past was gone, and all that remained was the shell of the building itself—a hazard, an eyesore, something to be torn down and replaced.

Chase's boots echoed on the wood floor. He led her along the edges, pointing at holes closer to the center. She wondered if any of his employees had caused the holes, walking imprudently across the floor, foot catching on the weak spot, and then slipping through.

He was taking her to the employees' staircase in the back. When they reached it, she saw why. It was made of metal. Rusted metal, but metal all the same. Someone had recently bolted the stairs into the wall, probably under Chase's orders. A metal hand railing had been reinforced as well.

Chase looked over his shoulder to make sure she was following. She caught a glimpse of something in his face—reluctance? Fear? She couldn't quite tell—and then, as suddenly as it appeared, it was gone.

He went down the steps two at a time. She followed. Even though the handrail had been rebolted, the metal still flaked under her hand. The bolts might hold if she suddenly fell through the stairs but she wasn't sure if the railing would.

The smell grew stronger here, as if the mold had somehow managed to survive the dry summers. The farther down she went, the cooler the air got. It was still hot, but no longer oppressive.

Chase stopped at the bottom of the stairs. He watched her come down the last few, his gaze holding hers. The intensity of his gaze startled her. It was vulnerable, in a way she hadn't seen since their first year together.

Then he stepped away so that she could stand on the floor below.

The smell was so strong that it overwhelmed her. Beneath the mold and rot, there was something else, something familiar, something foul. It made the hair rise on the back of her neck.

"That way," Chase said, and this time she wasn't mistaking it. His voice was shaking. "I'll wait here."

She frowned at him, and then kept going. The floor here was covered in ceramic tile, chipped and broken, but sturdy. She wondered what was beneath it. Ground? Old-fashioned concrete? Wood? She couldn't tell. But the floor didn't creak here, and it felt solid.

A long wall hid everything from view. A door stood

open, sending in sunlight filled with dust motes, just like she remembered. Only there shouldn't be sunlight here. This was the basement, the miraculous swimming pool, the place that had helped make the End of the World famous.

She stepped through the door.

The light came from the back wall—or what had been the back. Chase's crew had destroyed this part of the building.

The basement of the End of the World was open to the air for the first time since it had been completed.

That strange feeling she'd had since she reached the bottom of the stairs grew. If the basement wasn't sealed, then the stench shouldn't have been so strong. The old air should have escaped, letting the freshness of the desert inside.

Some of the heat had trickled in, but not enough to dissipate the natural coolness. She stepped forward. The tile on the other side of the pool was hidden under mounds of dirt. The pool itself was half destroyed, but the cat which had done the damage wasn't anywhere near it. She could see the big tire tracks, scored deeply into the sandy earth, as if the cat itself had been stuck or if the operator had tried to escape in a hurry.

They had uncovered something. That much was clear. And she was beginning to get an idea as to what it was.

A body.

Given the smell, it had to have died here recently. Bodies didn't decay in the desert—not in the dry air and the sand. Inside a building like this, there might be standard decomposition, but considering how hot it had been, even that seemed unlikely.

She'd have to assume cause of death was suspicious because the body had been located here. And then she'd have to figure out a way to find out whose body it was.

She was already planning how she'd conduct her case when she stepped off the tile onto a mound of dirt, and peered into the gaping hole, and saw—

Bones. Piles of bones. Recognizable bones. Femurs, hip bones, pelvic bones, rib cages. Hundreds of human bones. And more skulls than she could count.

She rocked back on her heels, pressing her free hand to her face, the smell—the illogical and impossible smell—now turning her stomach.

A mass grave, of the kind she'd only seen in film or police academy photos.

A mass grave, anywhere from a hundred to seventy-five years old.

A mass grave, in Hope. She hadn't even heard rumors of it, and she had lived here all her life.

"Son of a bitch," she said.

"Yeah," Chase said from the stairs, "I couldn't agree more."

THEN

The screaming sent ripples through her. She couldn't complete the change. She couldn't even assume the color and texture of the brick.

Tears pricked her eyes. Tears, as big a giveaway as her hair, her fingers, her ears. Somehow, when she stopped the spikes, she stopped all her abilities.

Or maybe it was just the fear.

A door squeaked open, then boots hit the sidewalk. Polished boots with only a layer of black dust along the edge. Men's boots, not the dainty things Momma tried to wear.

She tried to will the shivering away, but she couldn't.

She couldn't move at all.

Not that she had anywhere to go.

She could only pray that he wouldn't look down, that he wouldn't see her, that she would be safe for just a little longer.

NOW

Becca stared at the hole. She couldn't even count all the skulls, rising like white stones out of the dirt. Not to mention the rib cages off to one side or the tiny bones lying in a corner, bones that probably belonged in a hand or a foot.

She couldn't do much on her own. But she could find out where that stink was coming from.

She turned around and headed for the stairs.

Chase tipped his hardhat back, revealing his dark eyes. "Where're you going?"

"To get some things from my evidence bag," Becca said.

"You're not going to call anyone, are you?" he asked.

She stopped in front of him. "I can't take care of this alone. You should know that."

He leaned against the railing, that assumed casual gesture which meant he was the most distressed. "This'll ruin me, Becca. Half my capital is in this place."

"You told me no good businessman ever invests his own money," she snapped, mostly because she was surprised.

He shrugged. "Guess I'm not a good businessman."

But he was. He had restored three of the downtown's oldest buildings, making them into expensive condominiums with views of the mountains. Single-handedly, he'd revitalized Hope's downtown, by adding trendy stores that the locals claimed would never succeed (yet somehow they did, thanks to the "foreigners," as the Californians were called) and restaurants so upscale that Becca would have to spend half a week's pay just to eat lunch.

"You knew I'd go by the book when you called me here," she said, more sharply than she intended. He'd gotten to her. That was the problem; he always did.

"I thought maybe we could talk. They're old bones. If we can get someone to recover them and keep it quiet—"

"How many workers saw this?" she asked. "Do you think they'll keep it quiet?"

"If I pay them enough," he said. "And if we move the bones to a proper cemetery."

"Is that what you think this is?" she asked. "A graveyard?"

"Isn't it?" He seemed genuinely surprised. "It was so far out in the desert when this place was built that it's possible —no, it's probable—that the memory of the graveyard got lost."

"I saw at least two ribcages with shattered bones, and several skulls looked crushed."

His lips trembled, and it was a moment before he spoke. "The equipment could have done that."

But he didn't sound convinced.

"It could have," she said. "But we need to know."

"Why?" he asked.

She looked over her shoulder. That patch of sunlight still glinted through the hole in the wall. The dust motes still floated. If she didn't look down, the place would seem just as beautiful and interesting as it always had.

"Because someone loved them once. Someone probably wants to know what happened to them."

"Someone?" He snorted. "Becca, the pool was put over a tennis court that was built at the turn of the 20th century. No one remembers these people. Only historians would care."

He paused, and she felt her breath catch.

Then he said, "This is my life."

He used a tone and inflection she used to find particularly mesmerizing. Once she told their couples therapist that with that tone, he could convince her to do anything, and that was when the therapist told her that she had to get out.

"It's a crime scene," Becca said, knowing that the argument was weak.

"You don't know that for sure, and even if it is, it's a hundred years old," he said.

"Then what's the smell?"

He frowned, clearly not understanding her.

"This is a desert, Chase. Bodies buried in dirt in a dry climate don't decay. They mummify."

He blinked. He obviously hadn't thought of that.

"And," she said, "even if they had decayed because of some strange environmental reason particular to this basement, they wouldn't smell after a hundred years."

That guarded expression had returned to his face. Only his eyes moved now.

"Maybe it's something small," he said. "A mouse, someone's lost cat."

She shook her head. "Smell's too strong, and over the entire building. If it were something small, the smell would have faded back when you broke open that wall."

"Not when it was dug up?" he asked, seeming surprised.

"No," she said. "Is that when you first smelled it?"

"That's when they called me."

They, meaning his crew. She frowned at him, wondering if he was going to blame them.

But for what? A smell?

She'd have to find the source before she made assumptions.

And that, she knew, was going to be hard.

THEN

A hand touched her shoulder. A human hand, warm and gentle. Another shivery ripple ran through her. She still had a shoulder; she hadn't gotten rid of that either. How silly she must look, plastered against the brick wall like a half formed younglin.

Screams still echoed. The shouts had died down, although sometimes they rose up altogether, like a group got excited about something.

"You're one of them, aren't you?"

Male voice, human, just as gentle as the hand. She couldn't stop shivering.

"I won't hurt you."

She resisted the urge to rotate an eye upwards, so that she could see more than the boot.

"But you better come with me before they find you."

That did startle her. Her eye moved before she could stop it. It formed above her shoulder. He jumped back slightly when her eye appeared, but his hand never left her skin, even though it was finally turning tannish-red like the brick.

She'd seen him before. Daddy had laughed with him in the good days. He had slicked-back hair and a narrow face and kind eyes.

He crouched beside her, and looked right at her eye, like it didn't bother him, even though she knew it did. He wouldn't've jumped like that if it didn't.

"Please," he said, "come with me. I don't know when they're coming back. And someone might see us. Please."

She had to form a mouth. Her nose remained, tucked against her stomach from when she'd formed a ball, but her mouth had disappeared when she had tried to take on the appearance of the wooden sidewalk.

It took all her strength to make the mouth come out near the eye, and from the look of disgust that passed over his face, she still didn't look right. Her hair was on the other side of her body, and her eye was just above her shoulder. The mouth had probably come out on what would have been her back if she put herself together right.

Right being human.

That's what Momma said.

Momma.

"Please," he said again, and this time, she heard panic in his voice.

"Stuck," she said.

"Oh, Christ." He looked up and down the street, then at the buildings across from it.

He seemed younger than she remembered, or maybe she was as bad at telling human ages as Momma was.

"How do we get you unstuck?" he asked.

She didn't know. She'd never been like this, not this scared, not all by herself.

She tried to shrug and felt her other shoulder form into the wood. A splinter dug into her skin, and her entire body turned red with pain.

"What a mess," he said, and she didn't know if he meant her or what was going on or how scared they both seemed to be.

She willed herself to let go, but she was attached to the brick, and she'd lost control of half her body functions. Daddy said fear would do that.

Whatever happens, baby, he'd say, *you have to trust us. You have to believe we'll get together again. Let that be your strength, so that you never, ever succumb to fear.*

But he'd been gone for a long time now. And Momma hadn't come back for her, even though people were screaming.

The man tried to pry a flat corner of her skin from the edge of the brick. She could feel the tug, saw his face scrunch up in disgust when he got to the sticky underneath part.

"How'd you get there?" he asked.

"Squinched," she said.

"Squinched." He didn't understand. And she spoke his language, she knew she did. She formed the right mouth, she'd been using the words for a long time now, and she knew how they felt inside her brain and out.

"Can you show me?" he asked. "Can you squinch onto my arm?"

She wasn't supposed to squinch to a human. Momma was strict about that. Like there was something bad about it, something awful would happen.

But something awful was happening now.

The screams...

"No," she said, even though that had to be a lie. Momma and Daddy wouldn't forbid something if she couldn't't've done it in the first place.

"God," he said, then looked down the street where the screams had come from. Where the shouts had grown more and more angry every time they rose up.

Right now, it was quiet, and she hated that more.

She hated it all.

"Stay here," he said.

He stood up, letting go of her shoulder. The warm vanished, and the fear rose even worse. Her other shoulder disappeared, and she felt the spikes, threatening to appear.

She had to close both eyes and will the spikes away.

When she opened the eyes, he was gone.

She moved the eyes all over her skin, looking for him, and she didn't see him at all.

The street was still empty, and too quiet.

Then, faraway, someone laughed. A mean, nasty, brittle laugh.

She folded her ears inside her skin, and willed herself flat, hoping, this time, that it would work.

NOW

Becca climbed the stairs, clinging to the handrail, the rust flaking against her palms. She had to call for help. At most, she needed a coroner, and probably a few officers just to search for the source of that smell.

But she felt guilty about calling. Chase used to talk about restoring the End of the World when she'd met him. He had brought her out here on their first date, even though she'd told him that she had explored the property repeatedly when she was a child.

Maybe they'd be able to keep this out of the paper, particularly if it turned out to be a graveyard or a dumping ground. But even that probably wouldn't happen.

The newspapers seemed to love this kind of story.

If she reported this, she would condemn Chase's

project to a kind of limbo. With so much capital invested, he probably couldn't afford to wait until the legal issues were solved.

She almost turned around to ask him how much time he could give them, but then she'd be compromising the investigation. For all she knew, there was a recently killed human beneath that dirt, and someone (Chase?) was using the old bones to hide it.

Then she shook her head. Not Chase. He was manipulative and difficult, moody and untrustworthy, but he wasn't—nor had he ever been—violent.

She sighed and continued up the stairs. Much as she wanted to help him, she couldn't. She had an obligation to the entire community.

She had an obligation to herself.

The wind hit her the moment she stepped outside. Bits of sand stung her skin, sticking to the sweat. Even with the sun, it now felt cooler out here because of that wind.

The construction workers watched her. She didn't know most of them; the town had grown too big for her to know everyone by sight like she had when she was a child. Many of these workers were Hispanic, some of them probably illegal.

Hispanics expected her to check their papers. She was supposed to do that too, although she never did. She didn't object to people who worked hard and tried to improve their lives.

With one hand, she tipped her hardhat back and nodded toward the workers. Then she opened the squad's driver's door, and winced at the heat which poured out at her. She leaned inside, unwilling to go into that heat voluntarily, and grabbed the radio's handset.

She paused before turning it on, knowing that even that momentary hesitation was a victory for Chase.

Then she clicked the handset and asked the dispatch to send Jillian Mills.

Jillian Mills was the head coroner for Hope and the surrounding counties. She actually worked the job full time, but her assistants were dentists and veterinarians, and one retired doctor.

"You want the crime scene unit?" the dispatch asked. It was standard procedure for a crime scene unit to come with the coroner.

"Not yet," Becca said. "I'm not sure what exactly we have here, except that it's dead."

Which was technically true, if she ignored all the crushed and broken bones.

"Tell her to hurry," Becca added. "It's hot as hell out here and there's a construction crew waiting."

That usually worked to get any city official moving. Lately, the "foreigners" had taken to suing the city if their emergency or official personnel delayed money-making operations, even for a day.

Chase would never do that—he knew that getting

along with the city helped his permits go through and his iffy projects get approved—but Becca still used the excuse.

She didn't want to be here any longer than she had to.

She stood, lifted her hardhat, and wiped the sweat off her forehead. Then she closed the door and leaned on it for a moment.

The End of the World.

She wondered if Chase had ever thought that the name might have been prophetic.

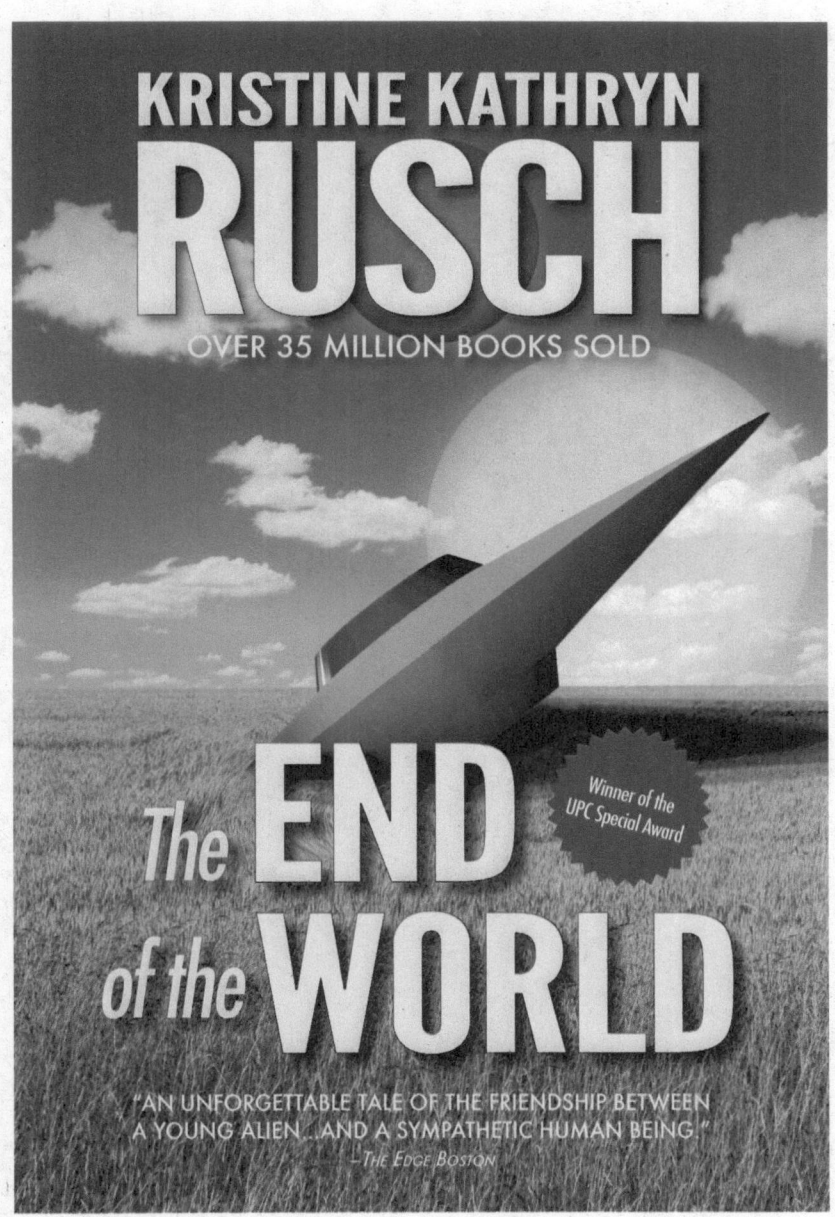

KRISTINE KATHRYN RUSCH

OVER 35 MILLION BOOKS SOLD

The **END** *of the* **WORLD**

Winner of the
UPC Special Award

"AN UNFORGETTABLE TALE OF THE FRIENDSHIP BETWEEN
A YOUNG ALIEN...AND A SYMPATHETIC HUMAN BEING."
—*THE EDGE BOSTON*

Keep Reading *The End of the World!*

Go to www.wmgbooks.com

HEAR DIRECTLY FROM KRIS

Sign up for the Kristine Kathryn Rusch newsletter and hear directly from Kris herself.

Go to kriswrites.com.

Get the latest news and releases from all of the WMG authors and lines, including Kristine Kathryn Rusch, Kristine Grayson, Kris Nelscott, Dean Wesley Smith, *Pulphouse Fiction Magazine, Smith's Monthly,* and so much more.

Go to wmgbooks.com.

You can also follow Kris on Bookbub.

We value honest feedback, and would love to hear your opinion in a review, if you're so inclined, on your favorite book retailer's site.

ABOUT THE AUTHOR

New York Times bestselling author Kristine Kathryn Rusch writes in almost every genre. Her novels have made bestseller lists around the world and her short fiction has appeared in eighteen best of the year collections. She has won more than twenty-five awards for her fiction, including the Hugo, Le Prix Imaginales, the Asimov's Readers Choice award, and the Ellery Queen Mystery Magazine Readers Choice Award.

Rusch writes in many genres, from science fiction to mystery, from western to romance. She has written under a pile of pen names, but most of her work appears as Kristine Kathryn Rusch. Her Kris Nelscott pen name has won or been nominated for most of the awards in the mystery genre, and her Kristine Grayson pen name became a bestseller in romance. Her science fiction novels set in the bestselling Diving Universe have won dozens of awards and are in development for a major TV show. She also writes the Retrieval Artist sf series and several major series that mostly appear as short fiction.

Rusch broke a number of barriers in the sf/f field, including being the first female editor of *The Magazine of Fantasy & Science Fiction*. She has owned two different publishing companies, and writes a highly regarded publishing industry blog on Patreon. She also writes a highly regarded weekly publishing industry blog. Find out more about her work at <u>kriswrites.com</u>, and more on all her books at wmgbooks.com.

facebook.com/kristinekathrynruschwriter

patreon.com/kristinekathrynrusch

bookbub.com/authors/kristine-kathryn-rusch